VIKING

An imprint of Penguin Random House LLC, New York

First published in the United States of America by Viking,
an imprint of Penguin Random House LLC, 2021

Visit us online at penguinrandomhouse.com.

Library of Congress Cataloging-in-Publication Data is available.

Manufactured in Spain

ISBN 9780593349830

1 3 5 7 9 10 8 6 4 2

EST

Design by Opal Roengchai
Text set in Chalkboard SE

Love from
MADELINE

Based on the character created by
LUDWIG BEMELMANS

Illustrations by
STEVEN SALERNO

VIKING

Love is being kind
to those we do not know.

Love is helping others

or your favorite pet

or someone who's upset.

You can show your love
with a gift

BON
ANNIVERSAIRE
MISS
CLAVEL
♡

or by giving someone else a lift.

Love is in the time you spend

on adventures with your friends.

But no matter where you roam,

love is always found at home.